For : My Mum ~ Mary Lavis

CALLUM

First published in the United Kingdom in 1999 by Ragged Bears Publishing Limited,
Milborne Wick, Sherborne, Dorset DT9 4PW

Distributed by Ragged Bears Limited, Ragged Appleshaw, Andover, Hampshire SP11 9HX
Tel: 01264 772269

Copyright © 1999 by Steve Lavis

The right of Steve Lavis to be identified as author and illustrator of this work has been asserted

A CIP record of this book is available from the British Library

ISBN 1 85714 178 4

Printed in Singapore

A Martha's Farm STORY

Toby the Runaway Tractor

by Steve Lavis

Quack!

Ragged Bears Publishing

One bright morning, Martha the farmer came bouncing round the corner on a little red tractor she had bought that day.

"Hello chickens!" said Martha, "Meet Toby, he's come to help on the farm."

Toby's first job was to move the chicken house.

Martha tied the house to the back of the tractor with some strong rope, she climbed up into the driving seat and Toby pulled the heavy, wooden chicken house slowly across the field.

"That's clever, Toby!" clucked all the chickens.

Toby felt very pleased with himself.

Next, Martha hitched up a small trailer to Toby and piled it high with clean straw for the pigs' bedding.

Toby didn't spill any straw as he went along the bumpy track.

"That's clever, Toby!" grunted all the pigs.

Toby was very pleased with himself.

Toby liked being useful on the farm and wanted to do more. So Martha loaded up the small trailer with two lambs and their mums.

The lambs had been born in the lambing shed and were now ready to go out into the field. Toby was very careful, and went around all the big holes in the lane so the sheep wouldn't bounce around too much.

"That's clever, Toby!" they bleated.

Toby thought he was too!

"That was easy!" thought Toby, "I hope we do something really hard next!" Martha also thought Toby was ready for something more difficult. So she hitched up the plough to the back of the tractor, and spent the rest of the

morning ploughing the biggest field on Martha's farm.

"That's clever, Toby!" mooed all the cows from over the hedge. Toby thought, "I'm the *cleverest* little red tractor that ever was!"

Moo!

Toby had rested while Martha had her lunch. This was a good thing because now Martha was making Toby pull the little trailer over the bridge that crossed the river and up the biggest, steepest hill on the farm.

"That's very clever, Toby!" neighed the horse as Toby puffed past her going up the hill. "You must be *very* strong!" When Toby reached the top of the hill he also thought, "I must be *very* strong! I must be the *cleverest and strongest* little red tractor in the whole world!"

They had driven up the steep hill to collect logs from the wood that grew at the top.

Toby was so busy thinking about what a clever and strong little red tractor he was that he had not taken much notice of the wood or the scarecrow standing close by, until it spoke to him...

"I've been watching you all day from up here on the hill. You can do so much; you must be very clever!" said Scarecrow.

"Yes I am," said Toby, "I am the cleverest and strongest tractor in the whole wide world!"

Oh no, come back!

All this time Martha had been busy, and the little trailer was now full of logs. "I'm just going to fetch my axe, and then we can go back down to the farm," said Martha.

"If I take the logs down the hill all by myself I can show Martha and all the animals how really clever, strong *and* special I am!" said Toby to Scarecrow.

"I don't think you should," said wise old Scarecrow, but it was too late... Toby had started to move...

At first the little red tractor
moved slowly, but soon he
started to roll faster and faster
down the steep hill!

LOOK
OUT!

shouted Martha as she ran from the woods....

LOOK OUT!

mooed the cows as they looked over the hedge...

LOOK OUT!

quacked the ducks,
as the little red tractor went...

Splash!

straight into the river at the bottom of the hill.

"That was *not* very clever!" Martha told Toby.

But all the animals thought Nell the horse was *very* clever as she pulled the shame-faced, *bright* red little tractor out of the river!

Martha did feel a little sorry for Toby, even though he had been foolish. "If you were so clever and could drive yourself, what would there be left for me to do?

Anyway, you needed a wash after all that ploughing!" Martha laughed, and the animals *and* Toby all joined in.